In

1935 if you wanted to
read a good book, you needed
either a lot of money or a library card.
Cheap paperbacks were available, but their
poor production generally mirrored the quality
between the covers. One weekend that year,
Allen Lane, Managing Director of The Bodley Head,
having spent the weekend visiting Agatha Christie,
found himself on a platform at Exeter station trying to
find something to read for his journey back to London.
He was appalled by the quality of the material he had to
choose from. Everything that Allen Lane achieved from that
day until his death in 1970 was based on a passionate belief
in the existence of 'a vast reading public for *intelligent*
books at a low price'. The result of his momentous vision
was the birth not only of Penguin, but of the 'paperback
revolution'. Quality writing became available for the price of
a packet of cigarettes, literature became a mass medium
for the first time, a nation of book-borrowers became a
nation of book-buyers – and the very concept of book
publishing was changed for ever. Those founding
principles – of quality and value, with an overarching
belief in the fundamental importance of reading –
have guided everything the company has
done since 1935. Sir Allen Lane's
pioneering spirit is still very much alive
at Penguin in 2005. Here's to
the next 70 years!

MORE THAN A BUSINESS

'We decided it was time to end the almost customary half-hearted manner in which cheap editions were produced – as though the only people who could possibly want cheap editions must belong to a lower order of intelligence. We, however, believed in the existence in this country of a vast reading public for intelligent books at a low price, and staked everything on it'
Sir Allen Lane, 1902–1970

'The Penguin Books are splendid value for sixpence, so splendid that if other publishers had any sense they would combine against them and suppress them'
George Orwell

'More than a business ... a national cultural asset'
Guardian

'When you look at the whole Penguin achievement you know that it constitutes, in action, one of the more democratic successes of our recent social history'
Richard Hoggart

The Great Wall of China

FRANZ KAFKA

PENGUIN BOOKS

PENGUIN BOOKS

Published by the Penguin Group
Penguin Books Ltd, 80 Strand, London WC2R ORL, England
Penguin Group (USA) Inc., 375 Hudson Street, New York, New York 10014, USA
Penguin Group (Canada), 10 Alcorn Avenue, Toronto, Ontario, Canada M4V 3B2
(a division of Pearson Penguin Canada Inc.)
Penguin Ireland, 25 St Stephen's Green, Dublin 2, Ireland
(a division of Penguin Books Ltd)
Penguin Group (Australia), 250 Camberwell Road, Camberwell, Victoria 3124,
Australia (a division of Pearson Australia Group Pty Ltd)
Penguin Books India Pvt Ltd, 11 Community Centre,
Panchsheel Park, New Delhi – 110 017, India
Penguin Group (NZ), cnr Airborne and Rosedale Roads, Albany,
Auckland 1310, New Zealand (a division of Pearson New Zealand Ltd)
Penguin Books (South Africa) (Pty) Ltd, 24 Sturdee Avenue,
Rosebank 2196, South Africa

Penguin Books Ltd, Registered Offices: 80 Strand, London WC2R ORL, England

www.penguin.com

Shorter Works, Volume 1 first published by Martin Secker & Warburg 1973
Published as The Great Wall of China and Other Short Works by Penguin Books 1991
The Transformation and Other Stories first published by Penguin Books 1992
This selection published as a Pocket Penguin 2005

1

Translations copyright © Malcolm Pasley, 1973, 1992
All rights reserved

The moral right of the translator has been asserted

Set in 11/13pt Monotype Dante
Typeset by Palimpsest Book Production Limited
Polmont, Stirlingshire
Printed in England by Clays Ltd, St Ives plc

Contents

The Great Wall of China   1

A Little Fable   21

The Knock at the Manor Gate   23

A Report to an Academy   25

Jackals and Arabs   39

The Next Village   45

The Vulture   47

Prometheus   49

The City Coat of Arms   51

Before the Law   53

The Great Wall of China

The Great Wall of China has been completed at its most northerly point. From the south-east and the south-west it came up in two sections that were united here. This system of piecemeal construction was also followed within each of the two great armies of labour, the eastern army and the western army. It was done by forming gangs of about a score of labourers, whose task it was to erect a section of wall about five hundred yards long, while the adjoining gang built a stretch of similar length to meet it. But after the junction had been effected the work was not then continued, as one might have expected, where the thousand yards ended; instead the labour-gangs were sent off to continue their work on the wall in some quite different region. This meant of course that many great gaps were left, which were only filled in by slow and gradual stages, and some indeed not until after the completion of the wall had actually been announced. It is even said that there are gaps which have never been filled in at all, and according to some people they are far larger than the completed sections, but this assertion may admittedly be no more than one of the many legends that have grown up round the wall, and which no single person can verify, at least not with his own eyes and his own judgement, owing to the great extent of the structure.

Now one might think at first that it would have been

more advantageous in every way to build continuously, or at least continuously within each of the two main sections. After all the wall was intended, as is commonly taught and recognized, to be a protection against the peoples of the north. But how can a wall protect if it is not a continuous structure? Indeed, not only does such a wall give no protection, it is itself in constant danger. These blocks of wall, left standing in deserted regions, could easily be destroyed time and again by the nomads, especially since in those days, alarmed by the wall-building, they kept shifting from place to place with incredible rapidity like locusts, and so perhaps had an even better picture of how the wall was progressing than we who were building it. Nevertheless the work could probably not have been carried out in any other way. To understand this one must consider the following: the wall was to be a protection for centuries; accordingly, scrupulous care in the construction, use of the architectural wisdom of all known periods and peoples, and a permanent sense of personal responsibility on the part of the builders were indispensable prerequisites for the work. For the meaner tasks it was indeed possible to employ ignorant day labourers from the populace, men, women, or children, anyone who was prepared to work for good money; but even for the supervision of four labourers an intelligent man with architectural training was necessary, a man who was capable of sensing in the depths of his heart what was at stake. And of course the higher the task, the greater the requirements. And such men were actually available, if not in the multitudes which this work could have absorbed, yet still in considerable numbers.

The work had not been undertaken lightly. Fifty years before the building was begun, throughout the whole area of China that was to be walled round, architecture, and masonry in particular, had been declared the most important branch of knowledge, all others being recognized only in so far as they had some connection with it. I can still well remember the occasion when as small children, hardly steady on our legs, we were standing in our teacher's garden and had to build a sort of wall out of pebbles, how the teacher tucked up his robe, charged at the wall, knocked it all down of course, and reproved us so severely for the feebleness of our construction that we ran off howling to our parents in all directions. A trivial incident, but indicative of the spirit of the time.

It was my good fortune that the building of the wall was just beginning when, at the age of twenty, I had passed the highest examination of the lowest school. I say good fortune, because many who before that time had reached the highest grade of the training available to them could for years put their knowledge to no purpose; they drifted around uselessly with the most grandiose architectural schemes in their heads and went to the bad in shoals. But those who were finally appointed to the great wall as overseers, even of the lowest grade, were really worthy of it. They were men who had reflected deeply on the wall and continued to reflect upon it, men who with the first stone which they sank in the ground felt themselves to some extent a part of it. But such men of course were not only eager to perform work of the greatest thoroughness, they were also fired with impatience to see the building finally erected in its full perfection. The day labourer knows nothing of this impatience, his wage is his only spur, and again the higher overseers, indeed even the overseers of middle rank, see enough of the manifold growth of the structure for it to keep them strong in spirit. But in order to encourage the men of lower rank, whose mental capacity far outstripped their seemingly petty task, other measures had to be taken. One could not, for instance, make them spend months or even years laying stone upon stone in some uninhabited mountain region hundreds of miles from their homes; the hopelessness of such laborious toil, to which no end could be seen even in the longest lifetime, would have reduced them to despair, and above all diminished their fitness for the work. It was for this reason that the system of piecemeal construction was chosen; five hundred yards could be accomplished in about five years, and indeed by that time the overseers were usually quite exhausted, they had lost faith in themselves, in the wall, in the world; but then, while they were still exalted by the festivities held to mark the uniting of the thousand-yard section, they were sent far away; on their journey they saw completed sections of the wall towering up here and there, they came past the quarters of higher commanders who presented them with decorations, they heard the cheers of new armies of labour streaming up from the depths of the provinces, they saw forests being felled to provide scaffolding for the wall, mountains being hammered into blocks of stone, in the holy places they heard the chants of the faithful praying for the wall's completion; all this soothed their impatience; the quiet life of their homeland, where they rested for a time, strengthened them; the esteem in which all builders were held, the humble credulity with which their accounts were listened to, the faith which the simple, peaceful citizens placed in the eventual completion of the wall, all this spanned the chords of the soul; like eternally hopeful children they bade farewell to their homeland, the desire to start work again on the great communal task became irresistible; they set off from home sooner than they need have done, half the village came out to keep them company until they were well on their way; on all the roads they were met with cheering, flags, banners; never before had they seen how vast and rich and fair and lovely their country was; each fellow-countryman was a brother, for whom one was building a protecting wall, and who returned his thanks for that throughout his life with all that he had and all that he was; unity! unity!, shoulder to shoulder, a great circle of our people, our blood no longer confined in the narrow round of the body, but sweetly rolling yet ever returning through the endless leagues of China.

Thus, then, the system of piecemeal construction becomes comprehensible; and yet there were probably other reasons for it as well. There is, by the way, nothing odd in my spending so long on this question; it is a crucial question for the entire building of the wall, however insignificant it may appear at first. If I am to convey an impression of the mental horizon and the experience of those days, and to make them intelligible, I simply cannot delve deeply enough into this particular question.

First of all one should recognize that the achievements

of those days were scarcely inferior to the building of the Tower of Babel, though as far as divine approval goes they represent, at least by human reckoning, the very opposite of that structure. I mention this because in the early stages of work on the wall a scholar wrote a book in which he drew the parallels in great detail. In it he attempted to prove that it was by no means for the reasons generally advanced that the Tower of Babel had failed to reach its objective, or at least that these well-known reasons did not include the most important ones of all. His proofs did not consist merely in written documents and reports; he also claimed to have made investigations on the spot, and to have discovered that the building failed, and was bound to fail, because of the weakness of its foundations. In this respect of course our own age had a great advantage over that long-past one; almost every educated contemporary was a mason by profession and infallible in the matter of laying foundations. But that was not at all what the scholar was driving at; instead he claimed that the Great Wall alone would create, for the first time in the history of mankind, a secure foundation for a new Tower of Babel. First the Wall, therefore, and then the Tower. His book was in everybody's hands at the time, but I must confess that I do not clearly understand to this day how he conceived the construction of that tower. How was the wall, which did not even form a circle, but only a sort of quarter or half-circle, supposed to provide the foundation for a tower? That could surely only be meant in a spiritual sense. But in that case what was the need for the wall, which was definitely something concrete, the result of the labour and the lives of hundreds of thousands of people? And why were there plans for the tower, admittedly somewhat nebulous plans, sketched in the book, and detailed plans set out for mobilizing the people's energies to undertake this new project? There was a great deal of confusion in people's minds at that time – this book is only one example – perhaps just because so many were doing their utmost to combine their forces in a single aim. The nature of man, flighty in its essence, made like the swirling dust, can abide no bondage; if it fetters itself it will soon begin to tear wildly at the fetters, rip all asunder – the wall, the binding chain, and itself – and scatter them to the four quarters of heaven.

It is possible that these considerations also, which in fact militate against the whole idea of building the wall, were not left out of account by the high command when the system of piecemeal construction was decided on. It was really only in spelling out the decrees of the supreme command that we – here I can probably speak for many – came to understand ourselves, and to discover that without our commanders neither our book learning nor our common sense would have been adequate even for the small task that fell to us within the great design. In the office of the high command – where it was, and who sat there, no one whom I have ever asked could tell me, either then or now – in that office there surely revolved all human thoughts and desires, and counter to them all human goals and achievements, while through the window the reflected glory of divine worlds shone in upon the hands of the commanders as they traced their plans.

And for that reason no impartial observer can believe

that the high command was not also capable of over-coming, if it had seriously wished to, the difficulties that stood in the way of building the wall continuously. One is forced to conclude, therefore, that the command deliberately chose the system of piecemeal construction. But piecemeal construction was only a makeshift and was inexpedient. So one is forced to conclude that the command willed something inexpedient. Strange conclusion, indeed; and yet from another point of view there is much justification for it. Today it is perhaps safe to speak of these things. In those days many of our people, and the best among them, had a secret principle which went as follows: Try with all your might to understand the decrees of the high command, but only up to a certain limit; then cease your reflections. A very wise principle, which moreover was further elaborated in a parable that has often been retold since: Cease from further reflection, but not because it might harm you; indeed it is by no means certain that it would harm you. It is not a question here of what is harmful or otherwise. It will happen to you as happens to the river in spring. It rises, it grows mightier, it gives richer nourishment to the land by the long reach of its banks, it retains its own character until it flows into the sea, it becomes ever more worthy of the sea and ever more welcome to it. – Thus far may you reflect on the decrees of the high command. – But then the river overflows its banks, loses outline and shape, slackens its course towards the ocean, tries to defy its destiny by forming little inland seas, damages the farmlands, yet cannot maintain itself at that width for long, but must run back again between its banks, indeed it must even dry up miserably in the hot season that follows. – Thus far do not reflect on the decrees of the high command.

Now while this parable may have been singularly pertinent during the building of the wall, it has at most only restricted application to my present account. For my own inquiry is a purely historical one; lightning no longer flashes from the thunderclouds that have long since rolled away, so I may venture to seek an explanation of the system of piecemeal construction which goes further than the one that contented people then. The limits which my powers of thought impose on me are narrow enough, but the province to be covered here is infinite.

Against whom is the Great Wall supposed to protect us? Against the peoples of the north. I come from the south-east of China. No northern tribe can threaten us there. We read about them in the books of the ancients; the cruelties which they commit in accordance with their nature make us heave deep sighs in our peaceful bowers; in the faithful representations of artists we see these faces of the damned, their gaping mouths, their jaws furnished with great pointed teeth, their screwed-up eyes that already seem to be leering at the prey which their fangs will crush and rend to pieces. When our children misbehave we show them these pictures, and at once they fling themselves sobbing into our arms. But that is all that we know of these northerners; we have never set eyes on them, and if we remain in our villages we shall never set eyes on them, even if they should spur their wild horses and keep charging straight towards us; the land is too vast and will never let them through to us, they will ride on until they vanish in the empty air.

Why then, since that is so, do we leave our native place, with its river and its bridges, our mothers and fathers, our weeping wives, our children who need our guidance, and go off for our training to the distant city, while our thoughts move on still further to the wall in the north? Why? Ask the high command. Our commanders know us. They, who are at grips with immense problems, know about us, know of our simple occupations, they can see us all gathered round in our humble dwellings, and the evening prayer that the father of the house recites in the family circle comes to their ears, to please them or to displease them. And if I may be allowed to express such ideas about the high command, I must say that in my opinion the high command was in existence earlier, and did not just assemble like some group of high mandarins, who at the prompting of a pleasant morning dream hastily summon a meeting, hastily pass resolutions, and drum the people out of their beds the same evening to carry the resolution out, even if it should be a mere matter of staging an illu-mination in honour of a god, who had smiled on them the previous day, perhaps only to belabour them in some dark corner the day after, almost before the lanterns are extinguished. My belief is rather that the high command has been in existence for ever, and the decision to build the wall likewise.

Already to some extent while the wall was being built, and almost exclusively ever since, I have occupied myself with the comparative history of peoples – there are certain questions whose most sensitive spot, so to speak, can only be reached by this method – and in the course of my studies I have discovered that we Chinese possess certain social and political institutions that are unique in their clarity, and again others that are unique in their obscurity. To explore the reasons for this, and particularly for the latter phenomenon, has always attracted me and still attracts me today, and these questions have a most important bearing on the building of the wall.

Now one of our most obscure institutions of all is unquestionably that of the empire itself. In Peking of course, especially in court circles, there does exist some clarity on the subject, though even that is more apparent than real; also the teachers of political law and history in the high schools claim to be exactly informed about these matters, and to be able to pass this knowledge on to their students; and the further down the ladder of the schools one goes, the more one finds, understandably enough, people's doubts of their own knowledge vanishing and a sea of semi-education rising mountain-high round a few precepts that have been rammed home for centuries – precepts which have indeed lost nothing of their eternal truth, but which also remain eternally unrecognized amid all the fog and vapour.

But on this question of the empire one should, in my opinion, turn first of all to the common people, since that is after all where the empire has its final support. Here I can admittedly only speak for my own home region. Apart from the nature gods and their ritual, which occupies the whole year in such variety and beauty, all our thoughts were turned solely to the emperor. But not to the current one; or rather they would have turned to the current one if we had known who he was, or anything definite about him. We too were of course always trying – it was the only curiosity that possessed us – to discover some information of this kind. But – strange as it may sound – it was scarcely possible to discover anything; not from the pilgrims, though they cover so much country, not from near nor from distant villages, not from the sailors, though they sail on the great sacred rivers as well as on our little stream. One certainly heard plenty, but from all that plenty nothing could be made out.

Our land is so vast, no fairy tale can give an inkling of its size, the heavens can scarcely span it. And Peking is only a dot, and the imperial palace less than a dot. But again the emperor, as such, is indeed mighty through all the many levels of the world. Yet the living emperor, a man like us, lies much as we do on a couch, which for all its generous proportions is still comparatively narrow and short. Like us he sometimes stretches his limbs, and when he is very tired, he yawns with his delicately cut mouth. How should we discover anything about that, thousands of miles away in the south, we who are almost on the borders of the Tibetan highlands? And besides, if any news should reach us it would come far too late, it would be long since out of date. Round the emperor there always presses the brilliant yet sinister throng of his courtiers, the counterweight to the imperial power, eternally striving to topple the emperor from his balance with their poisoned arrows. The empire is immortal, but the individual emperor falls and plunges down from the heights; even whole dynasties sink in the end, and breathe their last in a single death-rattle. Of these struggles and sufferings the people will never know; like latecomers, like strangers in a city, they stand at the far end of some densely packed side-street peacefully consuming the provisions they have brought with them, while far out in front of them, in the market square in the middle of the city, the execution of their ruler is proceeding.

There is a parable which expresses this relationship well. The emperor – so it is told – has sent to you, his solitary wretch of a subject, the minute shadow that has fled from the imperial sun into the furthermost distance, expressly to you has the emperor sent a message from his death-bed. He made the messenger kneel by his bedside and whispered the message to him; so much store did he set by it that he made him repeat it in his ear. With a nod of his head he confirmed the accuracy of the words. And before all the spectators of his death – every obstructing wall has been knocked away and on the towering open stairways there stand round him in a ring all the dignitaries of the empire – before all these has he dispatched his messenger. At once the messenger set out on his way; a strong, an indefatigable man, a swimmer without equal; striking out now with one arm, now the other, he cleaves a path through the throng; if he meets with resistance he points to his breast, which bears the sign of the sun, and he forges ahead with an ease that none could match. But the throng is so vast, there is no end to their dwellings; if he could reach open country how fast would he fly, and soon you would surely hear the majestic pounding of his fists on your door. But instead of that, how vain are his efforts; he is still only forcing his way through the chambers of the innermost palace, never will he get to the end of them; and if he succeeded in that, nothing would be gained; down the stairs he would have to fight his way; and if he succeeded in that, nothing would be gained; the courtyards would have to be traversed, and after the courtyards the second, outer palace; and again stairs and courtyards; and again a palace; and so on for thousands of years; and if at last he should burst through the outermost gate – but never, never can that happen – the royal capital would still lie before him, the centre of the world, piled high with all its dregs. No one can force his way through here, least of all with a message from a dead man to a shadow. But you sit at your window and dream up that message when evening falls.

Just so, just as hopelessly and as hopefully, do our people regard the emperor. They do not know which emperor is reigning, and there are even doubts as to the name of the dynasty. Many things of that kind are learnt by rote at school, but the universal uncertainty in such matters is so great that even the best pupils are affected by it. Emperors long since departed are raised in our villages to the throne, and one who only survives in song has recently issued a proclamation which the priest reads out before the altar. Battles of our most ancient history are fought now for the first time, and with glowing cheeks one's neighbour comes rushing into one's house with the news. The ladies of the emperors, overfed and sunk in their silken cushions, estranged from noble custom by wily courtiers, swollen with their lust for power, passionate in their greed, unbounded in their debauchery, perform their dreadful deeds ever anew; the more time that has passed, the more terrible the hues in which everything glows, and one day the village hears with loud lamentation how an empress, thousands of years ago, drank in long draughts the blood of her husband.

Thus, then, do our people behave towards the past emperors, but those of the present they mingle with the dead. If once, once in a lifetime, an imperial official on a tour of the provinces happens to arrive at our village, makes certain demands in the name of the ruler, examines the tax rolls, attends the school classes, questions the priest about all our doings, and then, before stepping into his litter, calls the whole community together and sums up his findings in a long speech of admonishment – then a smile will pass over all the faces, each man will steal a glance at his neighbour, people will bend over their children so as not to be observed by the official. Why, they think, he speaks of a dead man as if he were still alive; this emperor died long ago, the dynasty is extinct; the worthy official is making his sport with us, but we will behave as if we did not notice, so as not to offend him. But our serious obedience we shall give only to our present ruler; all else would be sinful. And behind the back of the official, as he is hurried away in his litter, some ruler who has been arbitrarily resurrected from a crumbling urn asserts himself with a stamp of his foot as lord of the village.

If one were to conclude from such phenomena that basically we have no emperor at all, one would not be far from the truth. Over and over again I must repeat: There is perhaps no people more faithful to the emperor than our people in the south, but our fidelity is of no benefit to the emperor. True, the sacred dragon stands on the little column at the end of the village, and from time immemorial it has been breathing its fiery breath in homage exactly in the direction of Peking; but for the people in our village Peking itself is far stranger than the next world. Can there really be a village where the houses stand side by side, covering more fields than can be seen from the top of our hill, and can crowds of people be packed between these houses day and night? Rather than to imagine a city like that, it would be easier for us to believe that Peking and its emperor were a single entity, say a cloud, peacefully voyaging beneath the sun through the course of the ages.

Now the result of holding such views is a life that is in a certain sense free and unconstrained. By no means immoral; such moral purity as exists in my native region I have scarcely ever met with on my travels. But it is a life that is subject to no law of the present, and obeys only the instructions and warnings reaching down to us from ancient times. I must beware of generalizing, and will not assert that this holds good for all the ten thousand villages of our province, far less so for all the five hundred provinces of China. But all the same I may perhaps be permitted, on the strength of the many works that I have read on the subject, as well as on the strength of my own observations – the building of the wall in particular, with its abundance of human material, afforded any man of feeling the opportunity to explore the soul of every province – on the strength of all this, then, I may perhaps be permitted to say that the attitude which prevails in

respect of the emperor has always and everywhere
certain basic features in common with the attitude in
my own village. However I do not at all wish to represent this attitude as a virtue; on the contrary. It is true
that the basic responsibility for it lies with the govern-
ment, which in this most ancient empire on earth has
been unable or else too preoccupied with other things
to develop imperial rule into an institution of sufficient
clarity for it to be immediately and continuously effec-
tive right to the furthest frontiers of the land. On the
other hand, however, this attitude also conceals a weakness of imagination or faith on the part of the people,
for they fail to draw out the imperial power from the
depths of Peking where it lies buried, and to clasp it in
its full living presence to their obedient breasts, while
at the same time they wish for nothing better than to
feel its touch upon them at last, and so be consumed.
So this attitude can hardly be considered a virtue. It is
all the more striking that this very weakness should
apparently be one of the most important unifying influ-
ences among our people . . .

Such was the world into which the news of the
building of the wall now penetrated. It too came belat-
edly, some thirty years after it had been announced. It
was on a summer evening. I, then aged ten, was standing
with my father on the river bank. As befits the importance of this much-discussed occasion I can recollect the
smallest details. He was holding me by the hand, something he loved to do into extreme old age, and was
running his other hand up and down his long, very thin
pipe, as though it were a flute. His long, sparse, stiff
beard was raised in the air, for as he smoked his pipe

he was gazing up into the heights beyond the river. At the same time his pigtail, object of the children's veneration, sank lower, rustling faintly on the gold-embroidered silk of his holiday robe. At that moment a bark drew up before us, the boatman signalled to my father to come down the embankment, while he himself climbed up towards him. They met halfway, the boatman whispered something in my father's ear; he put his arms round him to get really close. I could not understand what was said, I only saw that my father seemed not to believe the news, the boatman tried to assure him of its truth, my father still could not believe it, then the boatman, with the vehemence of sailor folk, almost ripped apart the clothes on his chest to prove the truth of his words, whereupon my father fell silent and the boatman leapt heavily into the bark and sailed away. Thoughtfully my father turned towards me, knocked out his pipe and stuck it in his belt, stroked me on the cheek and drew my head against his. That was what I liked best, it filled me with good spirits, and thus we returned home. There the rice-pap was already steaming on the table, a number of guests were assembled, the wine was just being poured into the goblets. My father paid no attention to any of this, and while still on the threshold he began to recount what he had heard. I cannot of course remember the exact words, but the sense impressed itself on me so deeply, owing to the exceptional nature of the circumstances that were enough to entrance even a child, that I do feel able to give some version of what he said. I do it because it was so very characteristic of the popular attitude. Well then, my father said something like this:

[A strange boatman – I know all those who usually pass here, but this one was a stranger – has just told me that a great wall is going to be built to protect the emperor. For it seems that infidel tribes, and demons among them, often gather in front of the imperial palace and shoot their black arrows at the emperor.]

A Little Fable

'Alas,' said the mouse, 'the world is growing smaller every day. At first it was so big that I was afraid, I ran on and I was glad when at last I saw walls to left and right of me in the distance, but these long walls are closing in on each other so fast that I have already reached the end room, and there in the corner stands the trap that I am heading for.' 'You only have to change direction,' said the cat, and ate it up.

The Knock at the Manor Gate

It was summer, a hot day. On my way home with my sister I was passing the gate of a manor-house. I cannot tell now whether she knocked out of mischief or out of absence of mind, or whether she merely threatened the gate with her fist and did not knock at all. A hundred paces further on along the high road, where it turned to the left, a village began. It was not a village we knew, but from the very first house people emerged, making friendly but warning signs to us; these people were terrified, bowed down with terror. They pointed to the manor we had passed and reminded us of the knock at the gate. The proprietors of the manor would charge us with it, the interrogation was to begin immediately. I kept quite calm and calmed my sister down as well. Probably she had not struck the gate at all, and even if she had, nowhere in the world would one be prosecuted for that. I tried to make this clear to the people around us; they listened to me but refrained from passing an opinion. Later they told me that not only my sister, but I too, as her brother, would be charged. I nodded and smiled. We all gazed back at the manor, as one watches a distant smoke-cloud and waits for the flames to appear. And sure enough, we presently saw horsemen riding in through the wide open gate; dust rose and obscured everything, only the points of their tall spears glittered. And hardly had the troop vanished into the main courtyard when they seemed to have turned their horses again and were on their way to us. I urged my sister to get away, I myself would set everything to rights; she refused to leave me on my own; then, I told her, she should at least change her clothes, so as to appear better dressed before these gentlemen. At last she obeyed and set out on the long road to our home. Already the horsemen had reached us, and from the saddle they began asking for my sister; she wasn't here at the moment, was the apprehensive reply, but she would be coming later. This response left them almost cold; the most important thing seemed to be that I had been found. The two chief members of the party were the judge, an energetic young man, and his silent assistant, whose name was Assmann. I was ordered into the parlour of the village inn. Slowly, swaying my head from side to side and hitching up my trousers, I set off under the watchful gaze of the party. I still half believed that a word would be enough to get me, the townsman, released – perhaps even honourably released – from this group of peasants. But when I had stepped over the threshold of the inn, the judge, who had hastened in front and was already awaiting me, said: 'I am sorry for this man.' And it was beyond all possibility of doubt that he was not referring to my present situation, but to what was about to happen to me. The room looked more like a prison cell than an inn parlour. Great stone flags, a dark-grey bare wall, an iron ring embedded somewhere in the masonry, in the middle something that was half pallet, half operating table.

A Report to an Academy

Esteemed gentlemen of the academy!

You have done me the honour of asking me to present a report to the academy concerning my past life as an ape.

I regret to say that I find myself unable to comply with your request as thus formulated. Almost five years now separate me from apehood, a short period, perhaps, as reckoned by the calendar, but an eternity to have to gallop through as I have done, accompanied along stretches of the course by excellent people, advice, applause and orchestral music, and yet essentially alone, since all such company remained – to pursue the metaphor – well on the far side of the rails. This achievement would have been impossible had I sought to cling wilfully to my origins, to the memories of my youth. It was precisely the renunciation of all self-will that I had laid upon myself as my first commandment; I, a free ape, submitted myself to this yoke. But as a result these memories, for their part, closed themselves off from me more and more. If initially a way of return lay open for me – had men so wished – through the whole great archway of the heavens that span the earth, this grew ever lower and narrower behind me as I was driven forward through the successive stages of my development; I felt ever more comfortable and secluded in the world of men; the storm sweeping after me from my past abated; today it is no more than a draught that cools my heels; and the distant hole through which it comes, and through which I once came, has become so small, that even if I had the strength and the will to run back so far, I should have to scrape the hide from my body to get through it. To speak plainly, much as I like using images for these things; to speak plainly: your own apehood, gentlemen, in so far as you have something of the sort behind you, cannot be further removed from you than mine is from me. Yet everyone who walks this earth feels a tickling at his heel: from the little chimpanzee to the great Achilles.

In the narrowest sense, however, I can perhaps make some reply to your inquiry after all, and indeed it gives me great pleasure to do so. The first thing I learnt was: how to shake hands; a handshake betokens frankness; allow me therefore today, as I stand at the summit of my career, to supplement that first frank handshake with the frankness of my present words. What I have to tell the academy will not amount to anything essentially new, and it will fall far short of what has been asked of me and what with the best will in the world I am unable to communicate – all the same, it should at least indicate the guideline that an erstwhile ape has followed, as he penetrated into the human world and established himself there. Yet I should certainly have no right to say even the little that follows unless I were entirely sure of myself, and if I had not achieved a position that is by now unassailable on all the great variety stages of the civilized world:

I come from the Gold Coast. For the account of my capture I have to depend on the reports of others. A hunting expedition from the firm of Hagenbeck – with whose leader, by the way, I have since consumed many a bottle of good red wine – was lying in wait in the scrub by the river bank when I came down to drink one evening, in the midst of a company. They fired at us; I was the only one that was hit; they got me twice.

Once in the cheek; that was a slight wound; but it left a large, bald, red scar, which earned me the repulsive and utterly inappropriate name of Red Peter – a positively apish invention, as if to suggest that the only thing distinguishing me from that performing ape Peter, a creature with some small reputation who met his end the other day, was this red mark on my cheek. But that is by the way.

The second shot got me below the hip; that was a bad wound; it is responsible for the fact that I still limp a little to this day. Recently I read an article, written by one of those ten thousand wind-bags who expatiate about me in the press, claiming that my ape nature was not yet wholly suppressed; the proof being that when visitors come to see me I am particularly inclined to take off my trousers so as to show them the spot where the bullet entered. That fellow ought to have each single finger of his scribbling hand shot away, one by one. I am permitted, I presume, to remove my trousers before anyone I please; nothing will be found there save a well-groomed coat of fur and the scar made – let us choose for this particular purpose a particular word, which should not however be misunderstood – the scar made by a heinous shot. Everything is open and above board; there is nothing to conceal; where the truth is at stake, every high-minded person will cast the refinements of behaviour aside. On the other hand if the writer of that article were to take off his trousers when visitors come, things would certainly appear in a different light, and I will let it stand to his credit that he does not. But in that case let him spare me in return with his delicacy!

After those shots I awoke – and this is where my own memories gradually begin – in a cage between decks aboard the Hagenbeck company steamer. It was no ordinary barred cage with four sides; instead it had three sides fastened to a crate; so the crate made the fourth side of the cage. The whole thing was too low to stand up in and too narrow to sit down. So I had to squat, with bent and constantly trembling knees, and furthermore – since at first I probably wished to see nobody, but just stay in the dark all the time – with my face turned towards the crate, while the bars of the cage cut into my flesh behind. Such a method of confining wild beasts is considered advantageous during the initial period, and today, after my own experience, I cannot deny that from the human point of view this is indeed the case.

But I did not think about that at the time. I had, for the first time in my life, no way out; certainly there was none straight ahead; straight ahead was the crate, plank fixed firmly to plank. Admittedly there was one gap running between them, which I greeted, when I first discovered it, with a howl of foolish rapture; but this gap was nowhere near big enough even to stick one's tail through, and no amount of an ape's strength could widen it.

Apparently, so I was told later, I made exceptionally little noise, from which they concluded that I was either on the point of extinction or that I would, supposing I managed to survive the first critical period, prove most amenable to training. I survived that period. Muffled sobbing, painful flea-hunting, weary licking of a coconut, beating my skull against the side of the crate, sticking out my tongue at anyone who came near – such were the first occupations of my new existence. But in all this just the one, single feeling: no way out. Of course what I then felt, in ape fashion, I can now only represent in human terms, and misrepresent it therefore; but even if I can no longer reach back to the old ape-truth, this does at least lie in the direction I have indicated, of that there is no doubt.

Up to now I had always had so many ways out, and now I had none. I was stuck fast. I would have had no less freedom of movement if they had nailed me down. And why was this so? Scratch yourself raw between the toes and you won't find the reason. Shove yourself back against the bar until it nearly cuts you in two and you won't find the reason. I had no way out; but I had to make one for myself, for I could not live without it. Always up against this crate – that would inevitably have been the end of me. But up against the crate is where apes belong with Hagenbeck – very well, then, I would cease to be an ape. A clear, a beautiful line of thought, one which I must have somehow hatched out in my belly, for that is the way apes think.

I fear that it may not be understood precisely what I mean by a way out. I use the term in its most ordinary and its fullest sense. I deliberately do not say freedom. I do not mean that grandiose feeling of freedom in all directions. Perhaps I may have known that as an ape, and I have come across men who yearn for it. But for my part it was not freedom that I sought, either then or now. Let me say in passing: freedom is all too often self-deception among men. And if freedom counts as one of the most sublime of feelings, equally sublime is the deception that corresponds to it. Many a time in variety theatres, waiting for my turn to come on, have I watched some pair of acrobats high up in the roof, performing on their trapezes. They swung, they rocked, they leapt, they floated into each other's arms, one carried the other in his teeth by the hair. 'This, too, is human freedom,' I thought, 'arbitrary movement.' What a mockery of mother nature! No building could withstand the laughter of the assembled apes at a sight like that.

No, freedom was not what I wanted. Only a way out; to right, to left, no matter where; I made no other demand; even if the way out should prove deceptive as well; the demand was small, the deception could be no greater. Onwards, onwards! Anything but stay still, with arms upraised, crushed against the side of a crate.

Today I can see it all clearly: without the profoundest inward calm I should never have got away. And indeed, perhaps I owe all that I have become to the calm that came over me after the first few days aboard ship. And for that calm, I might also well say, I had the members of the crew to thank.

They are a decent lot of people, when all is said and done. I can still recall with pleasure the sound of their heavy footsteps which used to echo through my head when I was half asleep. It was their habit to set about everything they did immensely slowly. If one of them wanted to rub his eyes, he would lift his hand like a dead weight. Their jokes were coarse but hearty. Their laughter always had a gruffness in it that sounded dangerous but meant nothing. They always complained that my fleas jumped over on to them; yet they were never seriously angry with me on that account; they knew, after all, that fleas flourish in my fur and that fleas are jumpers; so they came to terms with it. Sometimes when they were off duty a few would sit down in a semi-circle round me; hardly speaking, but making cooing grunts to one another; smoking their pipes, stretched out against the crates; slapping their knees as soon as I made the slightest movement; and now and then one of them would take a stick and tickle me where I liked being tickled. If I were invited today to make a voyage on that ship, I should certainly decline the invitation; but it is equally certain that not all the memories I might muse on between decks would be repellent ones.

Above all, the calmness that I acquired from the company of these folk prevented me from making any attempt to escape. When I now look back, it seems to me that I must have already had some inkling that I had to find a way out if I wanted to survive, but also that the way out was not to run away. I cannot tell any more whether flight was in fact possible, though I believe it was; flight should always be possible for an ape. With my teeth in their present state I have to be careful just cracking an ordinary nut, but then I should probably have managed in time to bite my way through the padlock on the door. I did not do it. What good would it have done me? As soon as I had poked my head out

I would have been recaptured, and locked away in some even worse cage; or I might have slipped unnoticed among some other animals, perhaps the boa constrictors opposite, and breathed my last in their arms; or I might even have succeeded in creeping up on deck and jumping overboard, in which case I would have been rocked for a little on the deep and then drowned. Desperate remedies. I did not work things out in such a human way, but under the influence of my surroundings I behaved as if I had.

I did not work things out; but I did observe everything with complete calm. I watched these men walking up and down, always the same faces, the same movements, often it seemed to me they were one and the same man. So this man or these men were moving about unmolested. A lofty goal began to dawn upon me. No one made me any promise that if I became like them the bars of my cage would be lifted. Such promises, for things that seem incapable of fulfilment, are not given. But make good the fulfilments and the promises will duly appear afterwards, just where you had earlier looked for them in vain. Now there was nothing about these men in themselves that particularly attracted me. Had I been a devotee of that freedom just mentioned, I would surely have preferred the ocean to the way out that I saw reflected in these men's dreary gaze. But anyhow I had been observing them for a long time before such things occurred to me, indeed it was only the accumulated weight of my observations that pushed me in the right direction.

It was so easy to imitate these people. I could spit after only a few days. Then we used to spit in one another's faces; the only difference was that I licked my face clean afterwards, they did not. I could soon smoke a pipe like an old hand; and if I also pressed my thumb down the bowl of the pipe, a roar of approval went up from the whole crew; only the difference between an empty pipe and a full one was something that took me a long time to understand.

What gave me the most trouble was the gin-bottle. The smell was a torture to me; I forced myself as best I could; but it took weeks for me to conquer my aversion. Strangely enough, the men took these inner struggles of mine more seriously than anything else. I cannot differentiate between these people even when I recollect, but there was one of them who came again and again, alone or with friends, by day, by night, at all kinds of hours; he would set himself down in front of me with the bottle and give me instruction. He could not make sense of me, he wanted to solve the riddle of my being. He would slowly uncork the bottle and then look at me to see whether I had understood him; I confess, I was always watching him with the wildest, the most precipitate attention; no such human pupil could any teacher hope to find on the whole surface of the earth; after the bottle was uncorked he would lift it to his mouth; I following him with my eyes right into his gullet; he nods, pleased with me, and puts the bottle to his lips; I, in an ecstasy of dawning enlightenment, scratch myself, amid squeals, here, there and everywhere at random; he is delighted, tips the bottle and takes a swig; I, impatient and desperate to emulate him, befoul myself in my cage, which again gives him great satisfaction; whereupon he, holding out the bottle at arm's length in front of him and returning it with a flourish to his lips, leans back with exaggerated pedantry and empties it at a single draught. I then, worn out by my excessive ambition, can follow him no longer and cling limply to the bars, while he completes the theoretical part of the lesson by stroking his belly and grinning.

And only now does the practical exercise begin. Am I not already all too exhausted by the theory? Indeed I am, all too exhausted. That is a part of my destiny. All the same I reach, as best I can, for the bottle that is held out for me; uncork it, trembling; with this success I feel my strength gradually returning; I lift the bottle, which by now I can hardly distinguish from the original; put it to my lips and – and fling it down with loathing, with loathing, although it is empty and contains nothing but the smell, fling it down with loathing to the floor. To the sorrow of my teacher, to the even greater sorrow of myself; nor do I succeed in placating either of us by the fact that I do not forget, even after throwing the bottle away, to stroke my belly in the most exemplary fashion and produce the accompanying grin.

All too frequently the lesson took this course. And to the credit of my teacher: he was not angry with me; sometimes, indeed, he may have held his burning pipe against my fur, until it began to smoulder in some place that I found hard to reach, but then he always extinguished it again himself with his massive, gentle hand; he was not angry with me, he recognized that we were both fighting on the same side against the nature of apes and that I had the harder task.

What a triumph it was then, both for him and for

me, when one evening before a large audience – perhaps it was some kind of party, a gramophone was playing, an officer was strolling about among the crew – when on this evening, just when no one happened to be looking, I seized a gin-bottle that had been left inadvertently in front of my cage, uncorked it in the approved manner, with the attention of the assembled company gradually mounting, put it to my lips, and without hesitation, without grimacing, like a professional drinker, with eyes rolling and throat gurgling, really and truly drank it dry; then threw the bottle from me, not in despair this time but with artistic skill; forgot, indeed, to stroke my belly; but instead, because I could not help myself, because I felt compelled, because all my senses were reeling, cried out a short, sharp 'Hallo!,' broke into human speech, sprang with this cry into the community of men, and felt their echoing cry: 'Listen, he's speaking!' like a caress over the whole of my sweat-drenched body.

I repeat: I felt no desire to imitate men; I imitated them because I was seeking a way out, and for no other reason. Nor did that first triumph take me far. My speaking voice failed again at once; it did not come back for months; my aversion to the gin-bottle returned even more strongly than before. But all the same, my course was now set for me, once and for all.

When I was handed over to my first trainer, in Hamburg, I soon grasped the two possibilities that were open to me: the Zoological Gardens or the variety stage. I did not hesitate. I told myself: do all in your power to get into variety; there lies the way out; the zoo is only another barred cage; if you land there you are lost.

And I began to learn, gentlemen. Oh yes, one learns when one has to; one learns if one wants a way out; one learns relentlessly. One watches over oneself with a whip; one flays oneself at the slightest sign of resistance. My ape nature went racing out of me, head over heels and away, so that my first teacher became himself almost apish in consequence; he soon had to abandon my instruction and be removed to a mental hospital. Fortunately he was soon discharged.

But I used up a great many teachers, indeed even several at once. When I had become more confident of my abilities, with the public already following my progress and my future beginning to look bright, I engaged instructors on my own account, established them in five communicating rooms and learned from them all simultaneously, by leaping continually from one room to the other.

The progress I made! Those rays of knowledge penetrating from every side into my awakening brain! I will not deny it: it gladdened my heart. But I must also admit: I did not overrate it, not even then, and how much the less do I do so today. By dint of exertions as yet unequalled upon this earth I have attained the cultural level of an average European. In itself that might be nothing to speak of, yet it is something, indeed, in so far as it has helped me out of my cage and provided me with this special kind of way out, the human way. There is an excellent idiom in German: to slip off into the undergrowth; that is what I did, I slipped off into the undergrowth. I had no other way to go, always provided that freedom was not to be my choice.

If I consider my development and the goal it has so

far reached, I can neither complain nor can I feel satis-
fied. With my hands in my trouser pockets, my bottle
of wine on the table, I half lie, half sit in my rocking-
chair and look out of the window. If a visitor comes, I
receive him politely. My manager sits in the ante-room;
when I ring he comes in and listens to what I have to
say. In the evening there is almost always a perform-
ance, and the success I enjoy would probably be hard
to surpass. When I come home late at night from
banquets, from scientific receptions, from informal
gatherings with friends, a little half-trained chimpanzee
is awaiting me and I enjoy her company after the fashion
of apes. By day I have no wish to see her; for she has
that wild, confused look of the trained animal in her
eye; no one but me can recognize it, and it is more than
I can bear.

On the whole I have at least achieved what I set out
to achieve. Let it not be said that it was not worth the
effort. In any case, I am not seeking anyone's judgement, I wish only to spread knowledge, I am only
reporting; to you, too, esteemed gentlemen of the
academy, I have only made a report.

Jackals and Arabs

We were encamped in the oasis. My companions were asleep. An Arab, a tall figure in white, strode past; he had been seeing to the camels and was going to his sleeping place.

I flung myself on my back in the grass; I wanted to sleep; I could not; the wailing howl of a jackal in the distance; I sat up again. And what had been so far off was suddenly close at hand. A seething mass of jackals around me; dull golden eyes gleaming out and fading away; lean bodies in orderly and nimble motion, as if controlled by a whip.

One came up from behind me, pushed through under my arm, pressing against me as if he needed my warmth; then he stepped almost eye to eye in front of me and spoke:

'I am the oldest jackal, far and wide. I am glad I'm still able to welcome you here. I'd almost given up hope, for we've been awaiting you for countless ages; my mother waited and her mother and every mother as far back as the first mother of all the jackals. Believe me!'

'I am surprised,' I said, forgetting to light the pile of firewood lying ready to keep the jackals off with its smoke, 'I'm very much surprised to hear it. I've only come down from the far north by chance, and I'm making a short journey. What is it you want then, jackals?'

And as if these words, perhaps all too friendly, had given them courage, they drew their circle closer round me; they were all breathing fast with a snarl in their throats.

'We are aware,' began the eldest, 'that you come from the north; that is just what we build our hopes on. People up there understand things that aren't understood by the Arabs down here. From their cold arrogance, I can tell you, no spark of understanding can be struck. They kill animals in order to eat them, and carrion flesh they despise.'

'Don't talk so loud,' said I, 'there are Arabs sleeping near.'

'You really must be a stranger here,' said the jackal, 'or you'd know that never in all history has a jackal been afraid of an Arab. Why, do you think we should be afraid of them? Is it not misfortune enough to be banished among such creatures?'

'Perhaps, perhaps,' said I, 'I don't presume to judge things so remote from my concerns; it seems to be a most ancient feud; so it probably runs in the blood; so maybe blood will be needed to end it.'

'You are very wise,' said the old jackal; and they all breathed even faster; their lungs straining, although they were standing still; a sour smell came from their gaping mouths which at times I had to grit my teeth to bear, 'you are very wise; what you say accords with our ancient teachings. So what we shall do is take their blood, and the feud is ended.'

'Oh!' I exclaimed, more vehemently than I meant to, 'they'll defend themselves; they'll shoot you down in packs with their muskets.'

'You misunderstand us,' said he, 'after human fashion, which seems to persist in the far north as well. Killing them is not at all what we have in mind. All the waters of the Nile would never suffice to wash us clean. The mere sight of their living flesh is enough to send us running off, out into a purer air, out into the desert which is therefore our home.'

And all the jackals standing round me, their number now increased by many others come up from afar, lowered their heads between their forelegs and polished them with their paws; it was as if they were trying to conceal their revulsion, a revulsion so terrible it made me want to leap clean out of their circle.

'What do you propose to do, then?' I asked, trying to get to my feet; but I was unable to do so; two young beasts behind me had fastened their teeth in my coat and my shirt; I had to remain seated. 'They are carrying your train,' explained the old jackal gravely, 'it's a token of respect.' 'They must let me go!' I cried, turning now to the old jackal, now to the youngsters. 'Of course they will,' said the old one, 'if you so wish. But it will take a little time, because as custom requires they have bitten in deep and first they must gradually loosen their jaws. Meanwhile, pray hear what we ask.' 'Your behaviour hasn't put me in a very receptive frame of mind,' I said. 'Don't hold our clumsiness against us,' said he, and now he began to make use of his natural wailing tone, 'we are only poor creatures, we have nothing but our teeth; we depend for all that we want to do, the good and the bad, on our teeth alone.' 'What is it that you want, then?' I said, only slightly appeased.

'Master,' he cried, and every jackal set up a howl; the

howling from the furthest distance seemed to reach my ears like a melody. 'Master, you are to end the strife that is dividing the world. You are exactly the man our ancients described as the one to accomplish it. We must be granted peace from the Arabs; air that we can breathe; the whole round of the horizon purified of their presence; never again the piteous cry of a sheep slaughtered with an Arab knife; every manner of beast must die in peace; we must be left undisturbed to drink them empty and cleanse them to the bone. Purity, purity is our sole desire' – and now all of them were crying and sobbing – 'how can you endure it in this world, you noble heart and sweet entrails? Filth is their white; filth is their black; a thing of loathing is their beard; the corner of their eye is enough to make you spit; and when they lift an arm, all hell gapes in their armpit. Therefore, O master, therefore, beloved master, with the help of your all-powerful hands, with the help of your all-powerful hands, take up these scissors and cut their throats!' And in obedience to a jerk of his head a jackal came trotting up, from one of whose corner-teeth there dangled a small pair of sewing scissors, covered in ancient rust.

'Right, so we've come to the scissors at last, and that's enough of it!' cried the Arab leader of our caravan, who had been creeping up to us against the wind and now cracked his gigantic whip.

All the jackals ran off in haste, but some distance off they stopped, cowering close together; the many beasts so stiff and tight-packed that it looked like a narrow hurdle, wreathed in flickering will-o'-the-wisps.

'And so, master, now you too have seen and heard

this spectacle,' said the Arab, laughing as heartily as the reserve of his race allowed. 'So you know what the creatures are after?' I asked. 'Of course, master,' said he, 'that's common knowledge; for so long as there have been Arabs these scissors have wandered the desert, and they will go on wandering with us until the end of time. Every European is offered the scissors to perform the great work; they imagine that every European is the very one called to perform it. They have an insane hope, these animals; they are fools, veritable fools. And we love them for it; they are our dogs; more beautiful ones than yours are. Now look, a camel has died in the night, I have had it brought along.'

Four bearers arrived and threw the heavy carcass down in front of us. Hardly had it touched the ground when the jackals raised their voices. As if they were drawn, each one, on a cord, irresistibly, they came hesitatingly forward, their bellies to the ground. They had forgotten the Arabs, forgotten their hatred; all else was obliterated by the presence of the reeking carcass that held them in its spell. One jackal was already hanging at the camel's throat and his first bite found the artery. Each muscle of his body twitched and jerked in its place, like a frenzied little pump that is utterly and hopelessly committed to the quenching of a raging fire. And by now they all lay piled up high on the carcass, each one labouring away.

Then out lashed the leader with his biting whip, fiercely to and fro across their backs. They raised their heads; still half numb in their ecstasy and stupor; saw the Arabs standing before them; now they were made to feel the whip on their muzzles; they sprang back and retreated a little. But already the blood of the camel was lying in pools, steaming high; in many places its body was torn wide open. They could not resist; back they came once more; once more the leader raised his whip; I caught hold of his arm.

'You are right, master,' he said, 'we will leave them to their task; besides, it's time to break camp. Now you have seen them. Wonderful creatures, aren't they? And how they do hate us!'

The Next Village

My grandfather used to say: 'Life is astonishingly short. When I look back now it is all so condensed in my memory that I can hardly understand, for example, how a young man can decide to ride over to the next village, without his being afraid – quite apart from unfortunate accidents – that the whole span of a normal happy life is far from being adequate for such a ride.'

The Vulture

A vulture was hacking at my feet. It had already torn my boots and stockings to shreds, now it was hacking at the feet themselves. Again and again it struck at them, then circled several times restlessly round me, then returned to continue its work. A gentleman passed by, looked on for a while, then asked me why I suffered the vulture. 'I'm helpless,' I said. 'When it came and began to attack me, I of course tried to drive it away, even to strangle it, but these animals are very strong, it was about to spring at my face, but I preferred to sacrifice my feet. Now they are almost torn to bits.' 'Fancy letting yourself be tortured like this!' said the gentleman. 'One shot and that's the end of the vulture.' 'Really?' I said. 'And would you do that?' 'With pleasure,' said the gentleman, 'I've only got to go home and get my gun. Could you wait another half hour?' 'I'm not sure about that,' said I, and stood for a moment rigid with pain. Then I said: 'Do try it in any case, please.' 'Very well,' said the gentleman, 'I'll be as quick as I can.' During this conversation the vulture had been calmly listening, letting its eye rove between me and the gentleman. Now I realized that it had understood everything; it took wing, leaned far back to gain impetus, and then, like a javelin thrower, thrust its beak through my mouth, deep into me. Falling back,

I was relieved to feel him drowning irretrievably in my blood, which was filling every depth, flooding every shore.

Prometheus

Four legends tell of Prometheus:

According to the first, he was clamped to a rock in the Caucasus for betraying the secrets of the gods to men, and the gods sent eagles to feed on his liver, which perpetually renewed itself.

According to the second, Prometheus, to escape the tearing beaks, pressed himself in his agony deeper and deeper into the rock until he became one with it.

According to the third, in the course of thousands of years his treachery was forgotten, the gods forgot, the eagles forgot, he himself forgot.

According to the fourth, everyone grew weary of what had become meaningless. The gods grew weary, the eagles grew weary, the wound closed wearily.

There remained the inexplicable mountain of rock. – Legend tries to explain the inexplicable. Since it emerges from a ground of truth, it must end in the inexplicable once again.

The City Coat of Arms

At first everything was tolerably well organized for the building of the Tower of Babel; indeed the organization was perhaps excessive, too much thought was given to guides, interpreters, accommodation for the workmen and roads of communication, just as if centuries of undisturbed opportunity for work lay ahead. It was even the general opinion at the time that one simply could not build too slowly; this opinion only needed to be over-emphasized a little and people would have shrunk from laying the foundations at all. The argument ran as follows: The essence of the whole enterprise is the idea of building a tower that will reach to heaven. Beside that idea everything else is secondary. The idea, once grasped in its full magnitude, can never vanish again; so long as there are men on earth there will also be the strong desire to finish building the tower. But in this respect there need be no anxiety for the future; on the contrary, human knowledge is increasing, architecture has made progress and will make further progress, in another hundred years a piece of work that takes us a year will perhaps be done in half a year, and what is more done better, more securely. So why be in such a hurry to toil away now to the limit of one's powers? There would only be sense in that if one could hope to erect the tower in the span of one generation. But that was quite out of the question. It seemed more likely that the next generation, with their improved knowledge, would find the work of the previous generation unsatisfactory, and pull down what had been built in order to start afresh. Such thoughts caused energy to flag, and people concerned themselves less with the tower than with constructing a city for the workmen. Each nationality wanted to have the best quarter; this gave rise to disputes, which developed into bloody conflicts. These conflicts continued endlessly; to the leaders they were a new proof that, since the necessary concentration for the task was lacking, the tower should be built very slowly, or preferably postponed until a general peace had been concluded. However the time was not spent only in fighting; in the intervals embellishments were made to the city, which admittedly provoked fresh envy and fresh conflicts. Thus the period of the first generation passed, but none of the succeeding ones was any different; except that technical skill was increasing all the while, and belligerence with it. To this must be added that by the time of the second or third generation the senselessness of building a tower up to heaven was already recognized, but by that time everybody was far too closely bound up with one another to leave the city.

All the legends and songs that have originated in this city are filled with the longing for a prophesied day, on which the city will be smashed to pieces by five blows in rapid succession from a gigantic fist. That is also the reason why the city has a fist on its coat of arms.

Before the Law

Before the law stands a doorkeeper. To this doorkeeper there comes a man from the country and asks to be admitted to the law. But the doorkeeper says that he cannot at present grant him admittance. The man considers, and then asks whether that means he may be admitted later on. 'It is possible,' says the doorkeeper, 'but not at present.' Since the gate leading to the law stands open as always and the doorkeeper steps aside, the man bends down to look through the gateway into the interior. When the doorkeeper sees this he laughs and says: 'If it tempts you so, then try entering despite my prohibition. But mark: I am powerful. And I am only the lowest doorkeeper. In hall after hall stand other doorkeepers, each more powerful than the last. The mere sight of the third is more than even I can bear.' The man from the country has not expected such difficulties; the law, he thinks, should be accessible to everyone and at all times; but as he now takes a closer look at the doorkeeper in his fur coat, at his large pointed nose, his long, sparse, black Tartar beard, he decides that it is better, after all, to wait until he receives permission to enter. The doorkeeper gives him a stool and lets him sit down to one side of the door. There he sits for days and years. He makes many attempts to be admitted and wearies the doorkeeper with his entreaties. The doorkeeper often conducts little examinations with him, questioning him about his home and about much else; but they are impersonal questions such as dignitaries ask, and he always concludes by repeating once again that he cannot yet admit him. The man, who has equipped himself well for his journey, uses up all that he has, however valuable it is, in order to bribe the door-keeper. The latter always accepts everything, but saying as he does so: 'I only accept so you won't feel there's anything you haven't tried.' Throughout the many years the man observes the doorkeeper almost without inter-ruption. He forgets the other doorkeepers, and this first one seems to him the sole obstacle barring his admis-sion to the law. He curses his misfortune, fiercely and loudly in the early years; later, as he grows old, he merely grumbles away to himself. He becomes childish, and since during his long study of the doorkeeper he has even discovered the fleas in his fur collar, he begs the fleas as well to help him and change the doorkeeper's mind. Finally his sight begins to fail and he does not know whether it is really growing darker around him or whether his eyes are just deceiving him. But he can indeed perceive in the darkness a radiance that streams out unquenchably from the doorway of the law. Now he has not much longer to live. Before his death all the experiences of the long years assemble in his mind to form a question which he has never yet asked the door-keeper. He beckons to him since he can no longer raise his stiffening body. The doorkeeper has to bend down to him, for the difference in height has changed very much to the man's disadvantage. 'What is it that you still want to know?' asks the doorkeeper, 'you are in-satiable.' 'Surely everyone strives to reach the law,' says the man, 'how does it happen that for all these many years no one except me has ever asked for admittance?' The doorkeeper recognizes that the man is at his end, and in order to reach his failing ears he raises his voice and bellows at him: 'No one else could ever have been admitted here, since this entrance was intended for you alone. Now I am going to close it.'

POCKET PENGUINS

1. Lady Chatterley's Trial
2. **Eric Schlosser** Cogs in the Great Machine
3. **Nick Hornby** Otherwise Pandemonium
4. **Albert Camus** Summer in Algiers
5. **P. D. James** Innocent House
6. **Richard Dawkins** The View from Mount Improbable
7. **India Knight** On Shopping
8. **Marian Keyes** Nothing Bad Ever Happens in Tiffany's
9. **Jorge Luis Borges** The Mirror of Ink
10. **Roald Dahl** A Taste of the Unexpected
11. **Jonathan Safran Foer** The Unabridged Pocketbook of Lightning
12. **Homer** The Cave of the Cyclops
13. **Paul Theroux** Two Stars
14. **Elizabeth David** Of Pageants and Picnics
15. **Anaïs Nin** Artists and Models
16. **Antony Beevor** Christmas at Stalingrad
17. **Gustave Flaubert** The Desert and the Dancing Girls
18. **Anne Frank** The Secret Annexe
19. **James Kelman** Where I Was
20. **Hari Kunzru** Noise
21. **Simon Schama** The Bastille Falls
22. **William Trevor** The Dressmaker's Child
23. **George Orwell** In Defence of English Cooking
24. **Michael Moore** Idiot Nation
25. **Helen Dunmore** Rose, 1944
26. **J. K. Galbraith** The Economics of Innocent Fraud
27. **Gervase Phinn** The School Inspector Calls
28. **W. G. Sebald** Young Austerlitz
29. **Redmond O'Hanlon** Borneo and the Poet
30. **Ali Smith** Ali Smith's Supersonic 70s
31. **Sigmund Freud** Forgetting Things
32. **Simon Armitage** King Arthur in the East Riding
33. **Hunter S. Thompson** Happy Birthday, Jack Nicholson
34. **Vladimir Nabokov** Cloud, Castle, Lake
35. **Niall Ferguson** 1914: Why the World Went to War

POCKET PENGUINS

36. **Muriel Spark** The Snobs
37. **Steven Pinker** Hotheads
38. **Tony Harrison** Under the Clock
39. **John Updike** Three Trips
40. **Will Self** Design Faults in the Volvo 760 Turbo
41. **H. G. Wells** The Country of the Blind
42. **Noam Chomsky** Doctrines and Visions
43. **Jamie Oliver** Something for the Weekend
44. **Virginia Woolf** Street Haunting
45. **Zadie Smith** Martha and Hanwell
46. **John Mortimer** The Scales of Justice
47. **F. Scott Fitzgerald** The Diamond as Big as the Ritz
48. **Roger McGough** The State of Poetry
49. **Ian Kershaw** Death in the Bunker
50. **Gabriel García Márquez** Seventeen Poisoned Englishmen
51. **Steven Runciman** The Assault on Jerusalem
52. **Sue Townsend** The Queen in Hell Close
53. **Primo Levi** Iron Potassium Nickel
54. **Alistair Cooke** Letters from Four Seasons
55. **William Boyd** Protobiography
56. **Robert Graves** Caligula
57. **Melissa Bank** The Worst Thing a Suburban Girl Could Imagine
58. **Truman Capote** My Side of the Matter
59. **David Lodge** Scenes of Academic Life
60. **Anton Chekhov** The Kiss
61. **Claire Tomalin** Young Bysshe
62. **David Cannadine** The Aristocratic Adventurer
63. **P. G. Wodehouse** Jeeves and the Impending Doom
64. **Franz Kafka** The Great Wall of China
65. **Dave Eggers** Short Short Stories
66. **Evelyn Waugh** The Coronation of Haile Selassie
67. **Pat Barker** War Talk
68. **Jonathan Coe** 9th & 13th
69. **John Steinbeck** Murder
70. **Alain de Botton** On Seeing and Noticing